Team USA

Mexico City   New Delhi   Hong Kong

This book is dedicated to the following people, who made my own Olympic experience in 1996 one to remember: Matt Williams, Brett Meister, David Griffin, Joe Soehn, Molly Mahoney, Peter Martin, Sandra Gage.

PHOTO CREDITS:
NBA Photos
Cover (Garnett, Houston, Payton, background), 3, 4, 20, 21, 22, 23, 24, 29: Andrew D. Bernstein.
Cover (Duncan, Kidd), 5 (Baker): Jesse D. Garrabrant. **5 (Payton):** Scott Cunningham. **12:** Barry Gossage. **8:** Rocky Widner.
6: Sam Forencich. **7, 9:** Glenn James. **10, 14:** Jon Hayt. **11, 28:** Nathaniel S. Butler. **13:** Garrett Ellwood. **15:** TK. **16:** TK.
17: TK. **18:** Bill Baptist. **19:** Fernando Medina. **26:** NBA Photo Library.

If you purchased this book without a cover, you should be aware that this book is stolen property. It was reported as "unsold and destroyed" to the publisher, and neither the author nor the publisher has received any payment for this "stripped book."

No part of this work may be reproduced, or stored in a retrieval system, or transmitted in any form or by any means, electronic, mechanical, photocopying, recording, or otherwise, without written permission of the publisher. For information regarding permission, write to Scholastic Inc., Attention: Permissions Department, 555 Broadway, New York, NY 10012.

The USA Basketball identifications reproduced in this publication are the trademarks, copyrighted designs and other forms of intellectual property of USA Basketball and may not be used, in whole or in part, without the prior written consent of USA Basketball. All rights reserved.

The NBA and individual NBA member team identifications, photographs and other content used on or in this publication are trademarks, copyrighted designs and other forms of intellectual property of NBA Properties, Inc. and the respective NBA member teams and may not be used, in whole or in part, without the prior written consent of NBA Properties, Inc. All rights reserved.

TEAM USA, TEAM USA 2000 and other Olympic marks and terminology are used with the permission of the United States Olympic Committee. 36 U.S.C. Sec. 220506

ISBN 0-439-15608-4

Copyright © 2000 USA Basketball
Copyright © 2000 NBA Properties, Inc.
All rights reserved. Published by Scholastic Inc.

SCHOLASTIC and associated logos are trademarks and/or registered trademarks of Scholastic Inc.

12 11 10 9 8 7 6 5 4 3 2 1   0 1 2 3 4 5 6/0

Printed in the U.S.A.
First Scholastic printing, June 2000
Book Design: Michael Malone

TABLE OF CONTENTS

MEET TEAM USA.................................4

VIN BAKER..6

TIM DUNCAN......................................7

KEVIN GARNETT.................................8

TOM GUGLIOTTA................................9

TIM HARDAWAY...............................10

ALLAN HOUSTON.............................11

JASON KIDD.....................................12

GARY PAYTON..................................13

STEVE SMITH...................................14

RAY ALLEN.......................................15

GRANT HILL.....................................16

ALONZO MOURNING.........................17

HEAD COACH RUDY TOMJANOVICH...........18

ASSISTANT COACHES.....................19

HOW THE DREAM TEAM CAME TO BE........20

A DREAM TEAM IS BORN................22

GOLD IN ATLANTA...........................24

USA BASKETBALL OLYMPIC HISTORY........26

WINNING MEMORIES.......................28

AROUND THE WORLD......................30

USA BASKETBALL OLYMPIC TRIVIA QUIZ...32

MEET TEAM USA

Earning a gold medal at the Olympic Games very simply means that you are the best in the world. It is the supreme athletic achievement for an individual and a triumph shared by millions of your fellow citizens. Winning the gold for your country is one of the greatest goals for athletes in all sports.

Basketball, a sport born and developed in the United States more than 100 years ago, has been a part of the Olympic Games since 1936. The United States has long displayed dominance in men's basketball, winning 11 gold medals in 13 tries at the Olympics.

In September, a team featuring some of the brightest stars in the NBA universe will try to uphold this glorious winning tradition at the 2000 Summer Olympic Games in Sydney, Australia. USA Basketball has selected 12 players for the team, and they include players of wondrous athletic ability and magnificent basketball skills.

Most coaches yearn for just one terrific point guard, a player who can make the game easier for all of his teammates and act as a coach on the floor. Instead of just one, Team USA 2000 has three of the best point guards in the world—Gary Payton, Jason Kidd and Tim Hardaway. Each can shoot the long jumper, score, pass and defend. They are three of the game's leading thinkers who provide their team with whatever it needs to be successful.

With the three-point arc in international competition just 20 feet, 6 inches from the basket, or three feet and three inches shorter than the NBA range, Olympic teams need shooters who can make long shots look as easy as a

Tim Duncan

Gary Payton

layup. That's why USA Basketball chose Allan Houston and Steve Smith, two of the sweetest-shooting athletes in the NBA.

In today's NBA, the best power players are not only large, but they are also fast and athletic. The days of the lumbering center are over. NBA big men can now not only use their size to get easy shots close to the basket, but they can also run up and down the court and keep up with the guards. On defense, they can rise up and swat down an opponent's shot with terrifying quickness and grace. This year, Team USA 2000 can call on the best of the best. The team's power players include the amazing Tim Duncan, whose all-around skills led the San Antonio Spurs to the 1999 NBA title in only his second NBA season; the astonishingly talented Kevin Garnett, who never met an alley-oop pass he couldn't dunk; Tom Gugliotta, who can use either his muscle or his exceptional outside shot without missing a beat; and Vin Baker, who can shoot like a smaller man but has the strength and size of any center.

The 12 NBA stars who make up the 2000 U.S. Olympic basketball team will be faced with the challenge of going up against the best the world can offer. There's no doubt they're determined to keep the gold right where it has been most of the time since basketball became an Olympic sport—the birthplace of basketball, the United States.

Vin Baker

VIN BAKER

Coaches love players like Vin Baker because of their versatility and unselfishness. Whether the team needs a clutch rebound, a momentum-changing blocked shot, or a good shot close to the basket, Vin can deliver the goods.

After spending the first four seasons of his career with the Milwaukee Bucks, Vin is now in his third season with the Seattle SuperSonics, playing alongside Olympic teammate Gary Payton. While in Milwaukee, Vin was named to the NBA All-Star Team in only his second season in the league. Since then, he's been an All-Star three more times, and is respected as one of the best power forwards in the NBA. Vin has averaged more than 18 points and nine rebounds in his NBA career.

With all that Vin has accomplished, it's amazing to think that just six years ago, he was a relatively unknown player from a small school, the University of Hartford. Since being the eighth pick in the 1993 NBA Draft, Vin has proven himself to be a big-time NBA player.

Born: 11/23/71
Height: 6-11 Weight: 250
College: University of Hartford
Drafted: #8, 1993, Milwaukee
NBA Career Averages:
18.1 points
9.0 rebounds
2.5 assists

TIM DUNCAN

Many great players in the NBA wait years before winning their first championship. Not Tim Duncan. He helped the San Antonio Spurs to the 1999 NBA title in only his second NBA season.

Several of the NBA's all-time greats have praised Tim for his work ethic and his terrific basketball fundamentals. That dedication, plus his ability to score, rebound, and block shots, have made him one of the NBA's best players. Tim was named to the All-NBA First Team in each of his first two seasons, and added to his honors by being named the Most Valuable Player of the 1999 NBA Finals. The most incredible part of Tim's story—he's only 24 years old.

Growing up in the Virgin Islands, Tim never thought he would be a professional basketball player. As a teenager, his goal was to become a world-class swimmer, and he was one of the best in his age group. But when he was 13, a hurricane destroyed the pool Tim used for swimming practice, so he turned to basketball, and went on to a spectacular career at Wake Forest, where he was a two-time All-America player as a college student.

Born: 4/25/76
Height: 7-0 Weight: 255
College: Wake Forest
Drafted: #1, 1997, San Antonio
NBA Career Averages:
21.3 points
11.7 rebounds
2.52 blocked shots

KEVIN GARNETT

Who can swish a long jumper, throw down an electrifying slam dunk, pin an opponent's shot against the backboard, and smile and laugh while doing all three? It has to be Kevin Garnett.

The Minnesota Timberwolves' superstar loves to play basketball, and he doesn't mind showing his enjoyment to everyone who is watching him. That group seems to grow by the day as Kevin matures into one of the very best players in the NBA. Despite being only 24 years old, Kevin has played in two NBA All-Star Games, and even his opponents have to admit he is one of the most exciting players to watch.

Even though Kevin is almost seven feet tall, he is as quick as players that are a foot shorter. When he is running in the open, it seems as if Kevin can take five big steps and cover the entire court! He uses his long arms and extraordinary jumping ability to swat down the other team's shots, and everyone agrees he is one of the best dunkers in the entire league. When he goes up for a dunk, every eye is on Kevin. How high will he go?

Born: 5/19/76
Height: 6-11 Weight: 220
High School: Farragut Academy (IL)
Drafted: #5, 1995, Minnesota
NBA Career Averages:
16.2 points
8.4 rebounds
3.3 assists

TOM GUGLIOTTA

Consistent rebounding demands a strong work ethic and plenty of desire. After all, the rebound doesn't always go to the player who jumps the highest, but to the player who uses his mind and body to get into perfect position to grab it, and who also simply wants the rebound more than the other guy.

Since Tom Gugliotta entered the NBA in 1992, he has given his team consistent rebounding. He's also a fine scorer, having averaged nearly 17 points per game for his career. But it is in his rebounding that you discover Tom's passion for the game. Googs is extremely aggressive and willing to grapple to get into the best position to grab the ball. Tom has led his team in rebounds in five of the seven seasons he has played in the NBA.

While rebounding is his forte, Googs is a well-rounded player who helps his team in many ways. He can shoot from the perimeter better than most men his size, and he is a good passer, taking the pressure off his team's point guards. Because of his unselfish ways, Tom has always been one of the most popular players everywhere he has played.

Born: 12/19/69
Height: 6-10 Weight: 240
College: North Carolina State
Drafted: #6, 1992, Washington
NBA Career Averages:
16.7 points
8.8 rebounds
3.6 assists

TIM HARDAWAY

Athletes heading to Sydney this September are thrilled to have the opportunity to represent their country in Olympic competition. But for Tim Hardaway, it means even more, because it's a second chance to represent the USA, which is something he thought might never come.

Tim has long been regarded as one of the best guards in the NBA, so it wasn't a surprise when he was picked for the USA Basketball team that was chosen to play in the 1994 World Championship in Canada. But in training camp for the 1993–94 NBA season, Tim suffered a serious knee injury and was forced to miss the entire season, as well as the World Championship.

But Tim called on the same fierce determination that made him an NBA All-Star before the injury, working diligently throughout his rehabilitation in order to once again take his place among the NBA's elite.

Tim not only made it back, he played well enough to be chosen to represent the United States in the 2000 Olympic Games. Tim proves it's true that if you are willing to work hard enough, almost anything is possible.

Born: 9/1/66
Height: 6-0 *Weight:* 195
College: Texas-El Paso
Drafted: #14, 1989, Golden State
NBA Career Averages:
19.4 points
3.6 rebounds
9.0 assists

ALLAN HOUSTON

The postseason is when sports heroes are born. When the white-hot spotlight of the playoffs shines brightly, teams look for those rare players who can take their game up a notch and play even better. Time and again, Allan Houston has proved to be a terrific player under pressure.

Allan's teams have made the playoffs four times in his six NBA seasons, and in each one of those seasons, Allan's scoring average in the playoffs has been even higher than it was during the season.

In the 1999 NBA Playoffs, the New York Knicks suffered the loss of star center Patrick Ewing to injury. The Knicks needed another player to make up for Ewing's absence. It was time for Allan to shine. Against Indiana, he scored 32 points in the win that propelled the Knicks into the 1999 NBA Finals against San Antonio.

Although the Knicks lost to the Spurs in the Finals, they won Game 3 when Allan scored a game-high 34 points. Allan led the Knicks in scoring in nine of their 20 postseason games in 1999.

Born: 4/20/71
Height: 6-6 *Weight:* 200
College: University of Tennessee
Drafted: #11, 1993, Detroit
NBA Career Averages:
15.3 points
2.8 rebounds
2.3 assists

11

JASON KIDD

Jason Kidd's teammates can't take their eyes off him. If they do, they risk getting hit in the chest with one of his incredible how-did-he-see-that passes. Teammates who want to take advantage of Jason's amazing court vision and quick passing ability know that paying attention to Jason means easy shots for them.

Most great players take over a game by scoring points. But Jason can take over a game in just about every way, even without scoring. He is able to see things before they happen on the court, allowing him to be one step ahead of the defense with his pinpoint passes. He seems to know what his opponents are thinking, which is why he is among league leaders in steals every season. Jason also has that rare sense of knowing the tempo of the game, another big benefit for his team.

Stronger than most guards he faces, Jason can always penetrate into the lane to create an easy shot for himself or a teammate. As a defender, Jason uses his strength to keep opposing point guards away from the basket. In so many ways, Jason controls the game, giving his team the best chance to win.

Born: 3/23/73
Height: 6-4 Weight: 212
College: Univ. of Cal.-Berkeley
Drafted: #2, 1994, Dallas
NBA Career Averages:
13.5 points
6.0 rebounds
9.1 assists

GARY PAYTON

Guess who NBA coaches say is one of the best post-up players in the league? No, it's not some 7-foot, 300-pound giant. It's Gary Payton, who is so slick and so strong around the basket, defenders don't have a chance to stop him before the ball is in the net.

But that's just one part of the game in which Gary excels. Gary is one of the best defensive guards in the history of the NBA. He's been named to the NBA All-Defensive First Team for six straight years! Bringing the ball into the frontcourt against Gary is a nightmare. His quick hands are constantly flicking for the ball, and once he tips it away from you, he's gone in a flash to the other end of the court for a layup.

On offense, Gary can shoot from downtown, but that's not his first choice. He likes to use his quick first step to the basket to blow by his man, draw other defenders to him, then pass to his teammates for easy shots. Gary can dribble the ball going full speed with either hand, making him almost impossible to guard. It's no wonder his opponents often have trouble sleeping the night before a game against Gary!

Born: 7/23/68
Height: 6-4 Weight: 190
College: Oregon State
Drafted: #2, 1990, Seattle
NBA Career Averages:
16.3 points
3.8 rebounds
6.8 assists

STEVE SMITH

You can call Steve Smith the answer man. He finds answers in every position he plays. When he first came into the league with the Miami Heat, his coaches asked Steve to play point guard, and he led the Heat in assists twice. When Steve was traded to the Atlanta Hawks, head coach Lenny Wilkens asked Steve to concentrate on scoring more points. So Steve led the Hawks in scoring for four straight seasons.

Last summer, Steve was traded to the Portland Trail Blazers. Whatever Portland wants him to do, it's certain that Steve will be up to the challenge. At a lanky 6-8, Steve uses his size to shoot over smaller guards. He is an excellent three-point shooter, and he also has the ability to beat defenders to the basket with his quickness. As a former point guard, Steve has great court vision, enabling him to spot open teammates. On defense, Steve can use his size and experience to defend forwards as well as guards.

Steve's versatility makes him a perfect player for the USA Basketball team. Whether it's scoring, passing or defense, Steve can do it all.

Born: 3/31/69
Height: 6-8 Weight: 221
College: Michigan State
Drafted: #5, 1991, Miami
NBA Career Averages:
17.4 points
3.9 rebounds
4.1 assists

RAY ALLEN

Pick any spot on the basketball court, and you are likely standing somewhere within Ray Allen's range. This Milwaukee Bucks guard has such a smooth stroke and can shoot the basketball so well that it's a surprise when the ball doesn't go in the basket. Ray practices his shot for hours every day during the off-season to make sure it continues to be a lethal weapon.

Some great shooters need time to get their feet set and find a good balance. But Ray seems to be able to catch a pass with these shooting essentials already taken care of. By the time he catches the ball, he's ready to let fly another perfect jumper from somewhere beyond the three-point line.

But Ray does a lot more than shoot. An excellent passer, Ray often starts a drive to the basket, only to drop the ball off to a teammate for an open shot. His unselfish nature makes it tough for opposing teams to defend him.

Ray doesn't just have basketball talent. His starring role in the Spike Lee film *He Got Game* showed that Ray has what it takes to excel off the court. But for now, Ray is ready to take center stage on the court with his teammates in Australia.

Born: 7/20/75
Height: 6-5 Weight: 205
College: University of Connecticut
Drafted: #5, 1996, Minnesota
NBA Career Averages:
16.6 points
4.4 rebounds
3.5 assists

GRANT HILL

Grant Hill is still a young player, although he has five NBA seasons in the bank. So why is his name already being mentioned with Hall of Famers like Wilt Chamberlain and Elgin Baylor?

In 1998–99, Grant led the Detroit Pistons in points, rebounds and assists for the third time in his career. In the history of the NBA, only all-time greats Wilt and Elgin have done this as many times as Grant. And he's only 27!

Grant is so smooth on the court that sometimes it seems as if the game is easy for him. But don't be fooled. Although Grant has been blessed with astonishing athletic ability, he constantly works hard to improve his game.

In his first six seasons, Grant has appeared in every All-Star Game and was named either First or Second Team All-NBA every year. He was named Schick NBA Co-Rookie of the Year along with Olympic teammate Jason Kidd in 1995. He was also an important member of the gold-medal-winning 1996 U.S. Olympic Team.

Even with his individual success, Grant is never satisfied unless his team comes out on top. That's why he wants to help Team USA win another gold.

Born: 10/5/72
Height: 6-8 Weight: 225
College: Duke
Drafted: #3, 1994, Detroit
NBA Career Averages:
20.7 points
8.1 rebounds
6.5 assists

ALONZO MOURNING

As they approach the age of 30, some players begin to see their abilities diminish. That's not the case with the powerful Alonzo Mourning. He just keeps getting better and better.

Alonzo was named NBA Defensive Player of the Year in 1999, partly because he led the NBA in blocked shots for the first time with 3.91 blocks per game. He was also named to the All-NBA First Team for the first time in 1999. This season, Alonzo had another terrific year, averaging career highs in scoring and blocked shots.

When Alonzo was drafted into the NBA in 1992, he realized that he was shorter than many of the NBA's top centers, but was determined not to let that stand in his way. Alonzo worked tirelessly to build his body into the sculpted mass of muscles it is today, while he retained the flexibility and athleticism that enables him to run fast and leap high to block shots.

Now Alonzo's game is an incredible combination of power and grace. He has the ability to score inside and outside, grab rebounds and play with so much enthusiasm that he energizes the entire Miami Heat team.

Born: 2/8/70
Height: 6-10 Weight: 261
College: Georgetown
Drafted: #2, 1992, Charlotte
NBA Career Averages:
21.0 points
10.2 rebounds
3.02 blocked shots

HEAD COACH RUDY TOMJANOVICH

Who better to coach a team of NBA superstars in the 2000 Olympic Games than the man who guides a team led by future Hall of Famers Hakeem Olajuwon and Charles Barkley? No one. That's one reason Rudy Tomjanovich of the Houston Rockets was entrusted with the responsibility of bringing home the gold medal in the 2000 Olympic Games.

Rudy earned the respect of the entire league when he led the Rockets to back-to-back NBA championships in 1994 and 1995. The Rockets were the only team besides the Chicago Bulls to win two NBA titles in the '90s.

Rudy has gained a reputation as an honest, fair coach, who has a great relationship with his players. A five-time NBA All-Star player himself during an 11-year playing career with the Rockets, Rudy knows what it takes to motivate some of the best players in the game. That's why he has the fifth-best winning percentage among active NBA coaches, having won more than 61 percent of his games (353–219, .617 winning percentage).

Rudy gained international coaching experience when he led a U.S. team of non-NBA players to the bronze medal at the World Championship of Basketball in 1998. With some of the NBA's brightest stars behind him this time, Rudy is ready to take on the world.

ASSISTANT COACH
LARRY BROWN

Ask any NBA coach for his list of the best teaching coaches in the league and Larry Brown's name will be near the top. With 27 years of experience as a head coach in the NBA, ABA and college, Larry has been a winner wherever he has coached. He won a national championship at Kansas in 1988, and turned losing teams into winning ones with the New Jersey Nets, San Antonio Spurs, Los Angeles Clippers and now with the Philadelphia 76ers. In 1999, Larry subbed for Rudy Tomjanovich and led the USA to a gold medal finish in the pre-Olympic Tournament of the Americas.

ASSISTANT COACH
GENE KEADY

Coaching excellence is synonymous with Purdue University's Gene Keady. A five-time National Coach of the Year and six-time Big Ten Conference Coach of the Year, Gene has guided the Boilermakers as head coach for 20 years, winning 70 percent of his games and leading his team to more than 400 wins. Purdue has won the Big Ten championship six times with Gene at the controls, and his teams have qualified for the NCAA Tournament 17 times. No stranger to the international game, Gene has guided four USA Basketball teams over the years and compiled an outstanding 22-2 record.

ASSISTANT COACH
TUBBY SMITH

Wherever Tubby Smith goes, success follows. Coach of the 1998 NCAA Champion Kentucky Wildcats, Tubby is the mentor of a program that sends players on to the NBA every season. He has had a dramatic impact on all three of the college teams where he has served as head coach. First, he rebuilt the program at the University of Tulsa, leading the team to a pair of NCAA Sweet Sixteen appearances. Then, in two seasons at the University of Georgia, he led the team to the first back-to-back 20-win seasons in school history. At the University of Kentucky, he guided the Wildcats to the title in his first season, and the team made it to the Elite Eight in 1999.

Larry Bird

HOW THE DREAM TEAM CAME TO BE

April 8, 1989, is one of the most important days in men's Olympic basketball history. No gold medals were won that day, and there wasn't even a basketball game played. That is the date that FIBA, the International Basketball Federation, voted in Munich, West Germany, by a 56–13 margin to allow all players in the world to play in international games, including the Olympics and World Championship of Basketball. Before that vote, the United States was represented only by college players at international events.

Some of the most enthusiastic supporters of the new rule were people from other nations. The international coaches, players and team officials knew that the NBA players were the best in the world. They knew that the only way they could ever hope to be as good as the NBA players was to play against them. So they were very happy when FIBA made it possible for NBA players to represent the United States in the 1992 Olympic Games in Barcelona.

The United States sent its best in 1992, a team led by three of the greatest in professional basketball history: Magic Johnson, Larry Bird and Michael Jordan. The rest of the team, coached by Chuck Daly, included the greatest NBA superstars, some of whom would prove to be among the best ever in the NBA. Charles Barkley, Karl Malone, David Robinson, Patrick Ewing, John Stockton, Scottie Pippen, Chris Mullin, Clyde Drexler and Christian Laettner joined the three legends to form what most believe was the greatest basketball team of all time.

Michael Jordan

A DREAM TEAM IS BORN

Chuck Daly, who had the honor of coaching the original Dream Team in 1992, said traveling with the team was like being on tour with The Beatles during their heyday in the 1960s. Each player was a superstar in his own right, a player who was on a first-name basis with sports' fans worldwide. Wherever the Dream Team went, whether it was at the Olympic Qualifying Tournament of the Americas in Portland, Oregon, the glittering beaches of Monte Carlo where the team trained, or the actual Games in Barcelona, thousands of screaming, cheering fans were on hand to join in the experience of the greatest basketball team ever assembled.

But sometimes in sports, having the most talented team doesn't always add up to victories. Even with the overwhelming talent present on the Dream Team, the players had to sacrifice and work together to achieve what they all wanted: an Olympic gold medal.

As it turned out, the Dream Team cruised through the eight games of the Olympics, defeating their opponents by a staggering average of nearly 44 points per game. Only in the gold medal game, a 117–85 victory over Croatia, did the Dream Team lead by less than 17 points at halftime. In that game, Michael Jordan made 10-of-16 shots and scored a team-high 22 points to lead the U.S. team to the gold medal. The Dream Team not only lived up to its billing as the greatest team of all time, it played with an unprecedented level of teamwork. Not one of the Dream Teamers averaged 20 points per game in the Olympics, while every player contributed to the team's success.

For the Dream Team members, their triumph meant their dreams of winning a gold medal for the United States had come true. But for millions of basketball fans around the world, the Dream Team meant a once-in-a-lifetime chance to see the best basketball team ever play at the highest level the game had ever seen. Marcelo Milanesio, an Argentinean guard and a star in his country and who played against the Dream Team in Portland, summed up the feeling of players who matched up with the Dream Team: "Not just for us but for everybody playing in this tournament, it is great to play with Michael Jordan and Magic Johnson," Milanesio said. "I am so overwhelmed with joy."

Magic Johnson

GOLD IN ATLANTA

The 1996 Summer Olympic Games in Atlanta are remembered for a tragic bombing, sweltering temperatures, and some of the best performances in history by athletes from the United States.

The 1996 U.S. Olympic Men's Basketball Team rose to the challenge and charged its way to an expected gold medal. But the aura that surrounded the original Dream Team, which captured the imagination of the sporting world in Barcelona in 1992, was not characteristic of this team. Opposing national teams, many with NBA players on the roster, were not in awe, and clearly were most interested in beating the team of NBA superstars who represented the United States.

"You can't match the first one. That was going to be special no matter what," said John Stockton, one of five Olympians who played on both the 1992 and 1996 teams. "The newness has worn off for the other teams, and maybe for us, too. The fact that the Dream Team is there doesn't magically change everybody into playing poorly or being awestruck against us."

Indeed, several national teams, including silver medal-winning Yugoslavia and Argentina, played the United States close for one half before the American team took over in the second half. The 1996 Dream Team won its eight games by an average margin of 31.8 points per game, certainly a sizable amount, but 12 points less than the margin for the 1992 Olympic Team. The rest of the world had a message for the United States: *We're better than we used to be and we're coming after you.*

"This year, it was like, 'Hey, we want to win,'" said Grant Hill. "So, I think it will definitely be tougher [to win the gold] in the future."

As in 1992, the United States did not rely on any one player to carry the scoring load since so many talented players were available to share the duties. David Robinson and Charles Barkley, two NBA superstars who also starred on the 1992 team, provided exceptional low post scoring when called upon. Shaquille O'Neal threw down a few intimidating dunks.

The versatility of the NBA players in Atlanta was the most evident reason why the rest of the world is still playing catch-up to the United States. Scottie Pippen, Penny Hardaway and Hill, three of the most gifted midsize players in basketball history, took turns applying the type of defensive pressure that players from the other national teams don't have to face regularly and only have nightmares about.

Reggie Miller and Mitch Richmond have few peers when it comes to shooting the perimeter jumper, and they found the shorter international three-point line used in the Olympics much to their liking. Miller was one of four U.S. players to have a point average in double figures, joining Robinson, Pippen and Barkley.

Gary Payton set the tone on defense and led the U.S. team in assists, while Stockton, Karl Malone and Hakeem Olajuwon, who realized a dream by playing for the U.S. team after completing the citizenship process, contributed big plays at key points. The unselfishness of the team was characterized by Olajuwon and Barkley, who each volunteered to sit out one of the early round games so that younger teammates could have more playing time.

Barkley, who had not expected to be asked to return to Olympic competition at the age of 33, captured the feeling of taking part in the Olympics. "It is an honor," said Barkley. "I was surprised to be asked to play, but this is something that is just too great to turn down. I consider it a privilege anytime you get a chance to represent your country."

1956 Olympic Team

USA BASKETBALL OLYMPIC HISTORY

Basketball was invented in the United States by Dr. James Naismith in 1891, and the sport grew rapidly in the United States through the early part of the 20th century. By the 1930s, the sport had spread throughout Europe and in South America, paving the way for the introduction of basketball as an Olympic sport in 1936. In fact, 23 nations sent basketball teams to compete in Berlin, Germany, in 1936!

The 1936 Olympic basketball competition was very different than it is now. The games were actually played on outdoor courts! The rules allowed teams to use a total of only seven players in a game (teams now consist of 12 players). The U.S. team won the gold medal game, defeating Canada, but they had difficult conditions. The game was not only played outdoors, but there was a heavy rainstorm.

There were no Olympics played in 1940 and 1944 because of World War II, but when they resumed in 1948, the U.S. showed it still had the best basketball team as it easily collected another gold medal.

During the next 20 years, the United States won five more gold medals, as a collection of spectacular talents made up the Olympic Team. In 1956, future NBA superstars Bill Russell and K.C. Jones of the University of San Francisco led the U.S. team to a gold medal by the incredible average victory margin of 53.5 points per game!

The 1960 team, believed by many to be the finest amateur team ever assembled, featured future Hall of Famers Oscar Robertson, Jerry West and Jerry Lucas. In 1964, Princeton star Bill Bradley and future NBA coach Larry Brown were teammates. In 1968, future NBA stars Spencer Haywood and Jo Jo White led the team to the gold. After the 1968 Olympics, not only had the U.S. won the gold medal in all seven Olympic basketball competitions it had entered, but the team had never lost a single game!

That changed in 1972. The U.S. team advanced to the gold medal game with only one real test, a seven-point win over Brazil. But in the gold medal contest, the United States lost a controversial 51–50 decision to the Soviet Union. The U.S. team's 63-game Olympic winning streak was over.

By the 1976 Olympics, the Soviet Union, Yugoslavia and several other countries had improved to the point that the United States was no longer an overwhelming favorite to win the gold. But coached by legendary Dean Smith and led by outstanding collegians Adrian Dantley, Phil Ford, Scott May, Mitch Kupchak and Quinn Buckner, the U.S. brought the gold back home.

The United States boycotted the 1980 Olympic Games, and the Soviet Union did likewise in 1984. The 1984 U.S. team, directed by Bobby Knight, included Michael Jordan, Patrick Ewing and Chris Mullin, and it easily swept the gold medal.

In 1988, the U.S. entered the Olympics as co-favorites with the Soviet Union, but when the two teams met in the semifinals, the Soviets took a hard-fought 82–76 win. The U.S. defeated Australia to take home the bronze medal.

It proved to be the last time a team of U.S. collegians competed for the gold medal. In 1989, the historic FIBA vote opened the door for NBA players to compete in the Olympics. A new era, in which all of the world's best players were allowed to compete for the gold, had dawned.

WINNING MEMORIES

John Stockton

1992 Olympic Team

"It was the most awesome feeling I ever had winning anything. The most exciting thing I've ever been through. When the national anthem was being played, I got goose bumps all over my body."
—Magic Johnson, after the United States won the gold medal in 1992.

"I've dreamed about watching that flag go up and hearing that national anthem my whole life. It was just awesome to experience it. It was well worth the broken leg, too."
—John Stockton, who suffered a fracture in his right leg during the Tournament of the Americas, but nonetheless played in four of the eight games in the Olympics.

"I can't explain the feeling up on that stand. We just won the gold medal for the whole U.S. I'm glad that everyone else on the team got to have the same feeling I had in 1984."
—Michael Jordan, who had been on the last gold medal-winning team of U.S. collegiate players in 1984.

"When my kids grow up, I can say I played in the Olympics and won the gold medal. It's a good way for me to go out as a winner."
—Larry Bird, who announced his retirement shortly after the conclusion of the 1992 Olympic Games.

Joe Dumars

1994 World Championship Team

"As a basketball player, I've won two NBA championships, and the rings and the trophies and all. But there's no such thing as a gold medal in my house. So the first thing that came to my mind was, 'This is an opportunity to win a gold medal.'"
—Joe Dumars, who hit 8-of-11 shots and scored 21 points to lead the team to the tournament-opening win over Spain.

"It meant a lot to play in an All-Star Game, but what makes this different is that you're representing not just a league, but your country. Basketball fans around the world view this like soccer fans view the World Cup."
—Mark Price, who drilled three-pointers from well beyond the international three-point arc throughout the competition.

"Any time you put USA across your chest, you're not playing for yourself or your team. You're playing for the little kids out there in their driveways playing basketball across America. So you can imagine my feelings when we won the gold medal and they played our national anthem."
—Reggie Miller, who hit eight three-pointers in the first half of the win over Puerto Rico.

"It was a long road. We wanted to show we were as dominant as Dream Team I. We wanted to dominate the championship game, that was important to us. We wanted to establish our own identity."
—Kevin Johnson, who helped lead the team to a convincing 137–91 victory over Russia in the gold medal game.

1996 Olympic Team

Grant Hill

"Wearing [the USA uniform] is the most wonderful feeling. It makes me feel like I have completed my journey. Playing with so many great players. Getting a chance to represent the country that has enabled my life to be so happy. If you wrote a book, you couldn't write it any better than this."
—Hakeem Olajuwon, who became a U.S. citizen just in time to compete as a member of the national team.

"I rank this [winning an Olympic gold medal] up there with winning an NBA championship. Those are two goals of mine, and so far I'm halfway there. This is a tremendous honor."
—Grant Hill, who gave his gold medal to his parents.

"It ranks number one in my career. There's no promise to have it again. It's unlike any other game of basketball. It's for your country, and you'll only have a group of guys like this together one time only. You have to cherish the moment."
—Penny Hardaway, who was second to Gary Payton on the 1996 Olympic Team in assists.

"You realize that you have a lot to uphold when you are playing for your country. As a player, I think you want to experience the jitters and the thrills from fans, and being able to walk away and say that you are part of history."
—Scottie Pippen, one of five players who played on gold medal-winning U.S. Olympic Teams in 1992 and 1996.

Past Olympic Games Basketball Results

(First place—gold, second place—silver, third place—bronze)

1936
1. United States
2. Canada
3. Mexico

1940 and 1944, no Olympics held due to World War II

1948
1. United States
2. France
3. Brazil

1952
1. United States
2. Soviet Union
3. Uruguay

1956
1. United States
2. Soviet Union
3. Uruguay

1960
1. United States
2. Soviet Union
3. Brazil

1964
1. United States
2. Soviet Union
3. Brazil

1968
1. United States
2. Yugoslavia
3. Soviet Union

1972
1. Soviet Union
2. United States
3. Cuba

1976
1. United States
2. Yugoslavia
3. Soviet Union

1980
(United States did not participate due to boycott of Olympics)
1. Yugoslavia
2. Italy
3. Soviet Union

1984
(Soviet Union, Cuba and Bulgaria did not participate due to boycott of Olympics)
1. United States
2. Spain
3. Yugoslavia

1988
1. Soviet Union
2. Yugoslavia
3. United States

1992
1. United States
2. Croatia
3. Lithuania

1996
1. United States
2. Yugoslavia
3. Lithuania

2000
1. _____
2. _____
3. _____

AROUND THE WORLD

At the 2000 Olympic Games this September in Sydney, Australia, 12 countries from around the world will gather their best players and shoot for the gold medal.

1. **Australia** *(Host Country)*

2. **Yugoslavia** *(1998 World Champions) (European Zone #3)*

3. **Angola** *(Africa Zone #1)*

4. **United States** *(Americas Zone #1)*

5. **Canada** *(Americas Zone #2)*

6. **China** *(Asia Zone #1)*

7. **Italy** *(European Zone #1)*

8. **Spain** *(European Zone #2)*

9. **France** *(European Zone #4)*

10. **Lithuania** *(European Zone #5)*

11. **Russia** *(European Zone #6)*

12. **New Zealand** *(Oceania Zone #1)*

USA BASKETBALL OLYMPIC TRIVIA QUIZ *(answers appear below)*

1. Name the two future Hall of Famers who tied as leading scorers for the 1960 U.S. Olympic Team.

2. Who led the original Dream Team in scoring at the 1992 Olympics?

3. Who was the head coach of the first U.S. Olympic Team in 1936?

4. Who is the only men's basketball player to have played in three Olympics for the United States?

5. Who was the leading rebounder on the 1972 U.S. Olympic Team?

6. Who was the head coach of the 1960 U.S. Olympic Team?

7. Name the member of the 1984 U.S. Olympic Team who later became an NBA referee.

8. Name the assistant coach of the 1992 Dream Team who was named head coach for the 1996 Olympics.

9. Name the member of the 1984 U.S. Olympic Team who is now a college head coach.

10. Which five players were members of both the 1992 and 1996 U.S. Olympic Teams?

1. Oscar Robertson and Jerry Lucas 2. Charles Barkley, who averaged 18 points per game 3. James Needles 4. David Robinson played in 1988, 1992 and 1996 5. Jim Brewer averaged 7.1 rebounds per game 6. Pete Newell 7. Leon Wood 8. Lenny Wilkens 9. Steve Alford 10. Charles Barkley, Karl Malone, Scottie Pippen, David Robinson and John Stockton